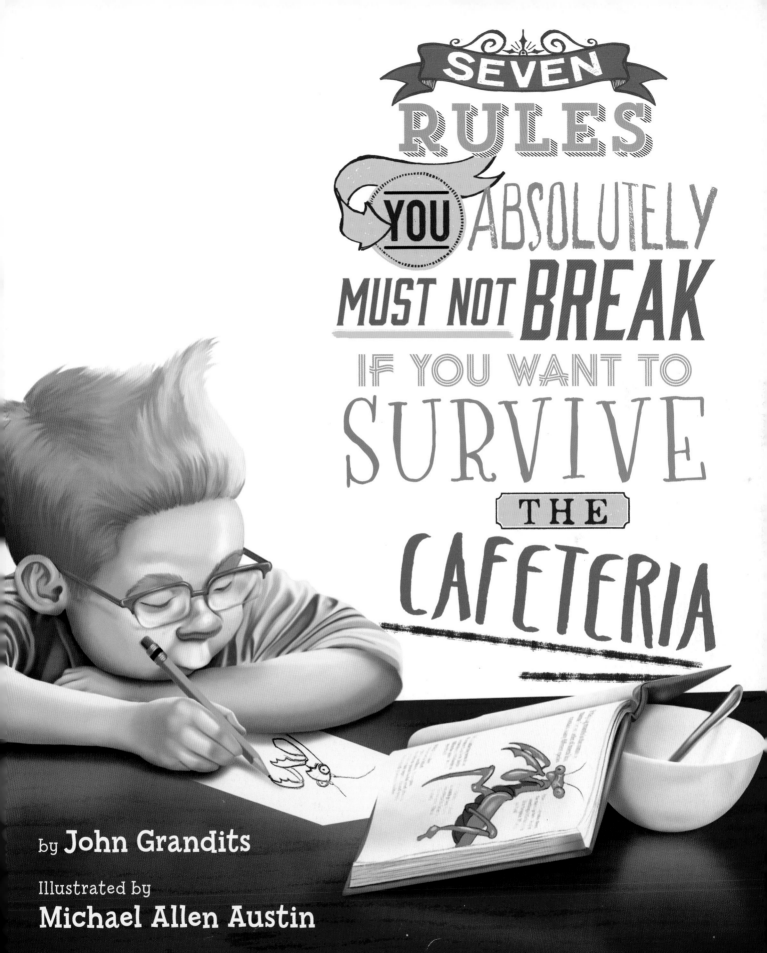

SEVEN RULES YOU ABSOLUTELY MUST NOT BREAK IF YOU WANT TO SURVIVE THE CAFETERIA

by **John Grandits**

Illustrated by
Michael Allen Austin

CLARION BOOKS | Houghton Mifflin Harcourt | Boston New York

For Rowan —J.G.

For Gloria, with a special thank-you to
Berkeley Lake Elementary for the inspiring
peek into their first-rate cafeteria
—M.A.A.

CLARION BOOKS
3 Park Avenue, New York, New York 10016
Text copyright © 2017 by John Grandits
Illustrations copyright © 2017 by Michael Allen Austin

Clarion Books is an imprint of Houghton Mifflin Harcourt Publishing Company.

www.hmhco.com

The illustrations in this book were executed in acrylic, colored pencil,
and digital on Strathmore 500 series illustration board.
The text was set in Billy Serif. | Design by Sharismar Rodriguez

Library of Congress Cataloging-in-Publication Data
Names: Grandits, John, author. | Austin, Michael Allen, illustrator.
Title: Seven rules you absolutely must not break if you want to survive
the cafeteria / by John Grandits ; illustrated by Michael Allen Austin.
Description: Boston ; New York : Clarion Books/Houghton Mifflin Harcourt,
[2017] | "A companion to Ten Rules You Absolutely Must Not Break
if You Want to Survive the School Bus." | Summary: Explains the rules
a kid must follow to survive the perilous world of the lunchroom.
Identifiers: LCCN 2015036598 | ISBN 9780544699519 (hardcover)
Subjects: | CYAC: Cafeterias—Fiction. | Rules (Philosophy)—Fiction.
Elementary schools—Fiction. | Schools—Fiction. | Humorous stories.
Classification: LCC PZ7.G76584 Se 2017 | DDC [E]—dc23
LC record available at http://lccn.loc.gov/2015036598

Manufactured in China | SCP 10 9 8 7 6 5 4 3 2 1
4500646578

It was Monday morning, and I was on the school bus, sitting next to Ginny. She's a class ahead of me, and she talks and talks and talks. Today she was talking about her lunch. How she likes carrots but thinks celery is too stringy. How rye bread is okay but only without seeds. How chocolate milk is better than plain, and squishy bananas are gross.

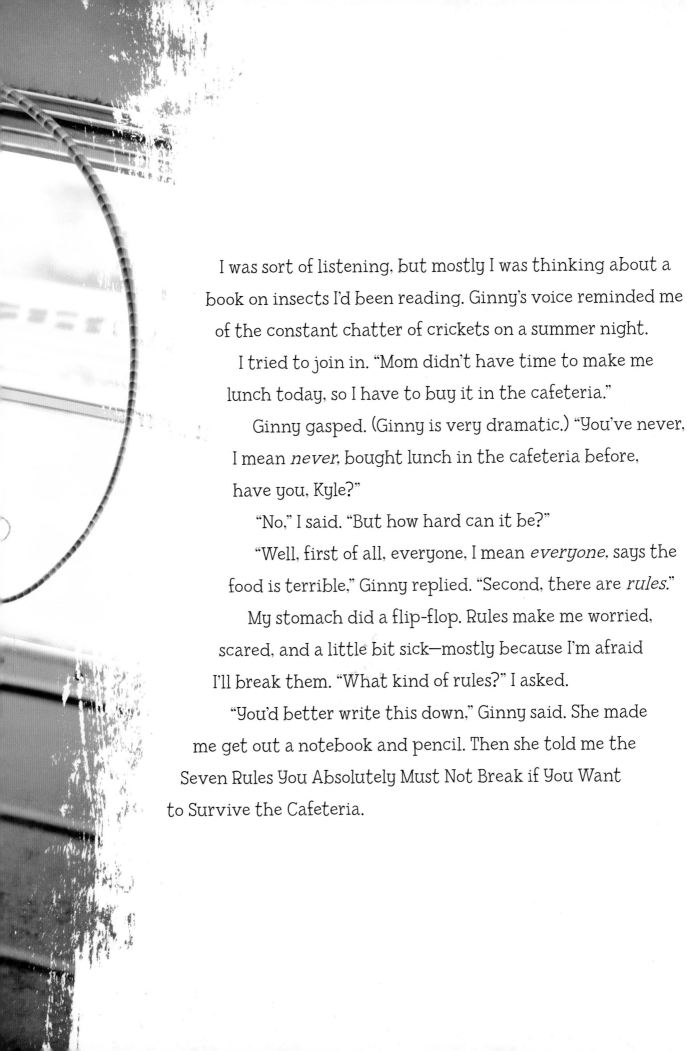

I was sort of listening, but mostly I was thinking about a book on insects I'd been reading. Ginny's voice reminded me of the constant chatter of crickets on a summer night.

I tried to join in. "Mom didn't have time to make me lunch today, so I have to buy it in the cafeteria."

Ginny gasped. (Ginny is very dramatic.) "You've never, I mean *never*, bought lunch in the cafeteria before, have you, Kyle?"

"No," I said. "But how hard can it be?"

"Well, first of all, everyone, I mean *everyone*, says the food is terrible," Ginny replied. "Second, there are *rules*."

My stomach did a flip-flop. Rules make me worried, scared, and a little bit sick—mostly because I'm afraid I'll break them. "What kind of rules?" I asked.

"You'd better write this down," Ginny said. She made me get out a notebook and pencil. Then she told me the Seven Rules You Absolutely Must Not Break if You Want to Survive the Cafeteria.

We got to school, and the morning went along as usual. Then, at
11:25, it was time for lunch. My class scurried down the hall like a
column of starving army ants.

I was last in line once we reached the cafeteria, and another class got in line right behind me. They were sixth graders, and they were as scary as a swarm of yellow jackets. I didn't turn around. It's best to ignore wasps. They sting when they're angry.

The lunch line inched its way forward. Finally, I reached a stack of trays and a sign that said TODAY'S MENU. I stopped to check it out. There was pasta and salad. There were chicken tacos and mini carrots. There were bananas and oranges and fruit cups. Awesome! I was trying to figure out what to choose when I felt a poke in my back. A hard poke.

I turned around. Oh, no! It was Arthur, a bully who rode the same school bus as me, and he didn't look happy. I felt like a little snail faced with a giant meat-eating water bug.

"Hey, dweeb!" he yelled. "Get moving. I'm hungry."

That's when I remembered the first thing Ginny had told me . . .

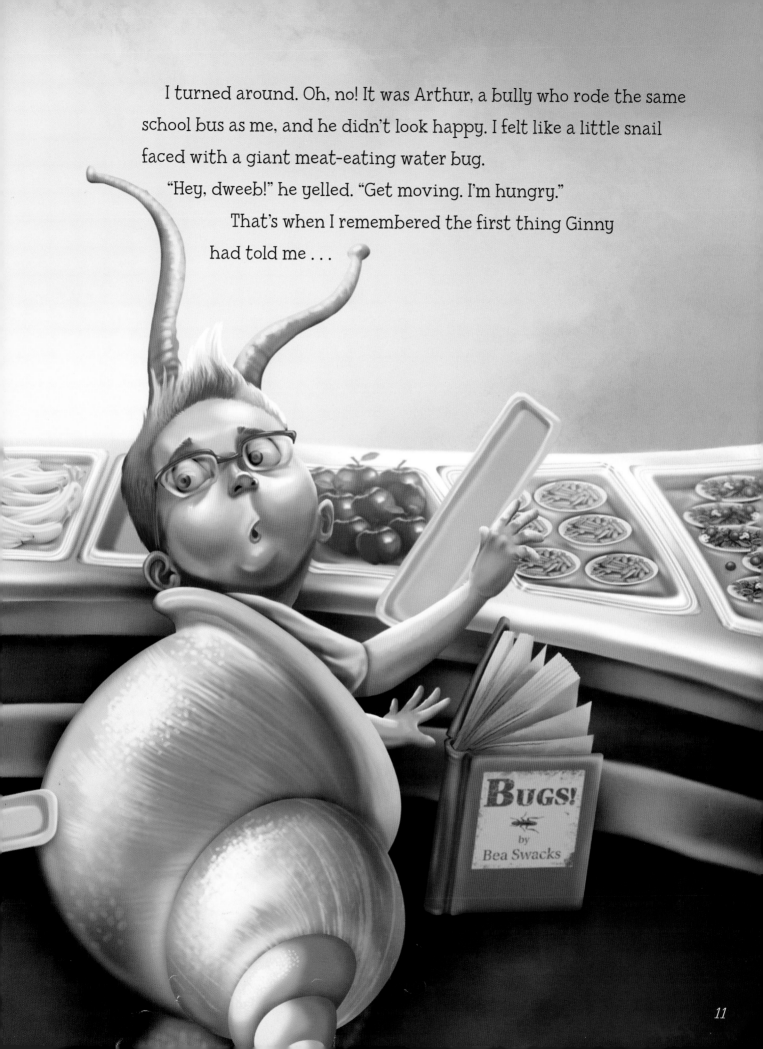

BUGS!
by
Bea Swacks

RULE ONE:

DON'T HOLD UP THE LINE.

The man who was serving the food gave my school-bus bully a look. "What's the racket, Arthur?" he said. "Is there a problem?"

"It's not his fault," I said quickly. "I was taking a long time to read the menu."

"Well, then, Arthur, just go around this young man," the server said.

The entire sixth-grade class went around me. At least *that* disaster was avoided.

I took a tray and got started. Everything looked so good, I took one of each. I was just cramming an extra carton of milk on my tray when the server said, "No, no, no. You can't have everything. You can only have one thing from each category."

Uh-oh! I'd completely forgotten . . .

RULE TWO:

DON'T TAKE TOO MANY THINGS.

Boy, was I embarrassed! I put back half the stuff.
Then I shot off toward the tables.

"Just a minute, sonny. I think you forgot
something," said a raspy voice behind me.
It was the lunch lady, who always circles
the cafeteria like a buzzing fly, looking for
troublemakers. That's when I realized I'd broken . . .

RULE THREE:

DON'T FORGET TO PAY.

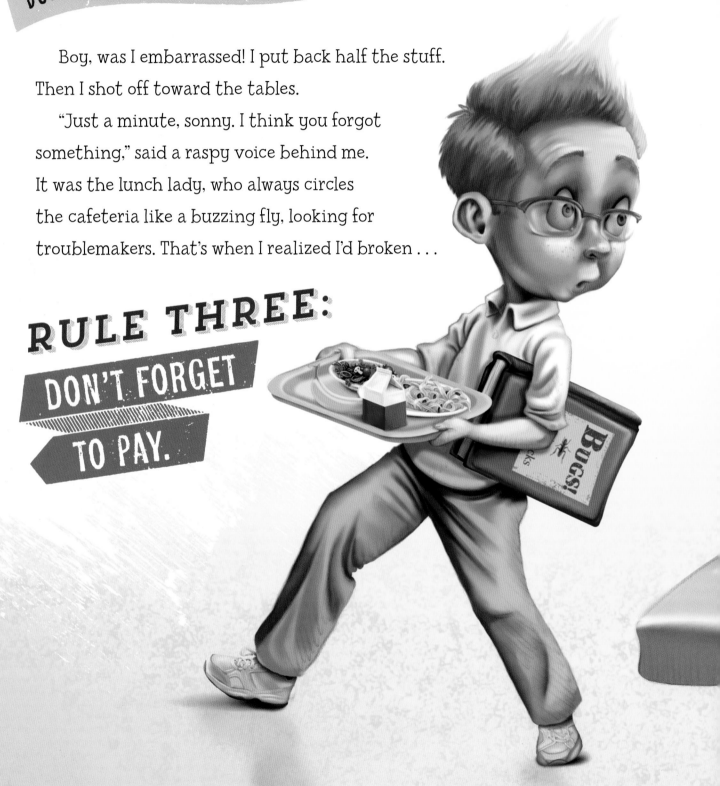

I dashed back to the register and tried to hand the cashier the five-dollar bill my mom had given me.

"You don't pay with money!" the cashier said. "When you get to the register, we type in your PIN number. Then the cost of your lunch is charged to your account." She peered at me. "You *do* know your PIN number, don't you? They gave it to you on the first day of school."

I didn't know my PIN. But the cashier was real nice and looked it up for me. Meanwhile, the next class had swarmed in. I was breaking Rule One again, and they were getting restless. Behind me, the growling and grumbling got louder and louder.

"Here you go. Your PIN number is eight-two-four-two," the cashier told me. "Just keep saying that over and over so you don't forget it."

"Eight-two-four-two. Eight-two-four-two," I repeated, and she waved me on. Finally I could go sit down and eat. I looked around the room because of . . .

RULE FOUR:

ALWAYS EAT WITH YOUR CLASSMATES.

There they were, way across the cafeteria. Oh, no! There was only one place left! I started running so I could get to it before someone else did.

That's when it happened. I tripped over my own feet! I fell flat on my belly, and the tray went flying. I couldn't believe it. I had just broken . . .

RULE FIVE:

HOLD ON TO YOUR TRAY.

Everyone around me shrieked—which brought the lunch lady swooping over. I picked up as much of the mess as I could. Then she led me back through the lunch line to get more food. The whole time, she lectured me about not running and not endangering myself and others. Buzz, buzz, buzz.

By the time the lunch lady let me go, the last seat
at my class's table was taken. I set down my tray and
tried to squeeze in anyway, but the other kids
started yelling about me pushing.

The fly lady was back in an instant. "That's it!
You've caused enough trouble for
one day," she said.

I hung my head. Ginny had
especially warned me
to obey . . .

RULE SIX:

NEVER AGGRAVATE THE LUNCH LADY.

She gave me another lecture. Then she said, "I want you to pick up your tray and walk very, very slowly to that table over there."

I couldn't believe it. I'd aggravated her three times in about thirty seconds. And now, as my punishment, she was making me break Rule Four. Even worse, the table she was sending me to was filled with sixth graders!

With the lunch lady's big, bulgy eyes watching me, I had no choice but to walk very, very slowly to the big kids' table. That's when I heard, "Hey, dweeb. C'mere. You can sit with me."

It was Arthur the bully. He was hunched over his food with five other meat-eating water bugs.

I sat down next to him. What else could I do?

"Thanks for covering for me in line," Arthur said. "If I got in trouble with that lunch guy one more time, I'd get sent to the principal's office for sure."

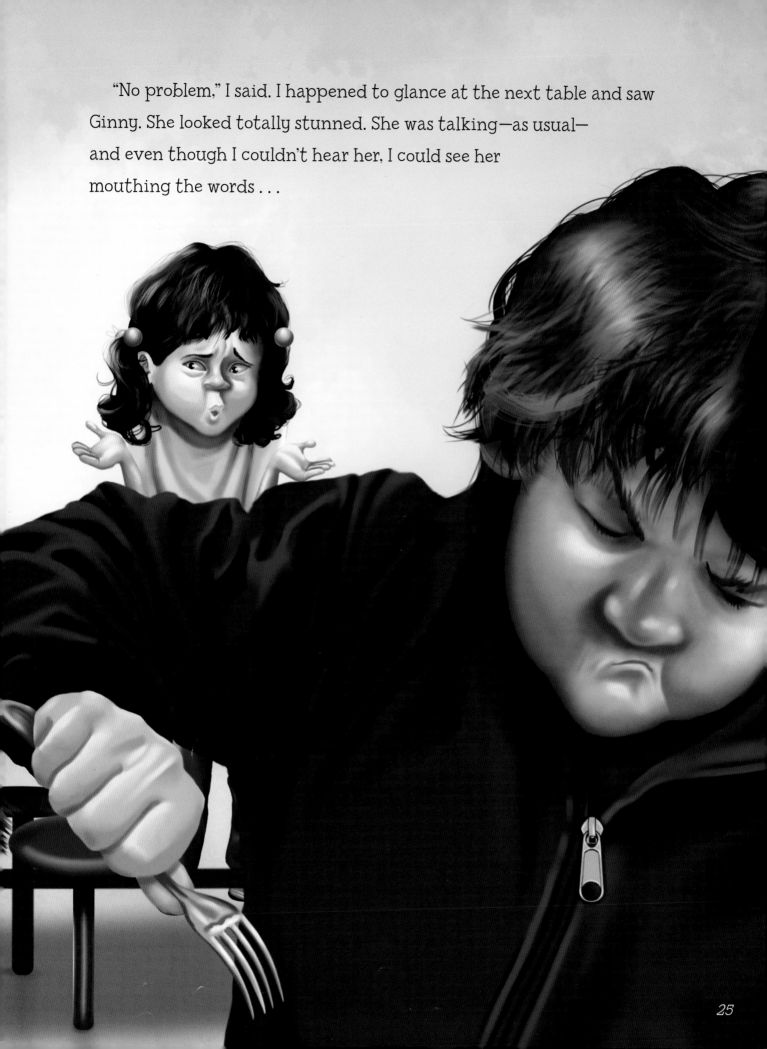

"No problem," I said. I happened to glance at the next table and saw Ginny. She looked totally stunned. She was talking—as usual—and even though I couldn't hear her, I could see her mouthing the words . . .

RULE SEVEN:

NEVER, EVER TALK TO THE BIG KIDS.

Okay, not all big kids are scary. My brother is a big kid, and he's a regular guy. But Arthur and his friends were terrifying! I couldn't meet their eyes, so I looked down at my pasta. The noodles reminded me of little worms. That made me think of my insect book again and of some of the cool facts I'd learned.

"Did you know that a cockroach can live without its head for nine days before it dies of starvation?" I said.

"Also, there's a wasp that lays its eggs in a caterpillar, and when they hatch, they eat it from the inside out.

And if you get a tapeworm in your intestines, it can grow up to fifty feet long."

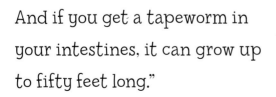

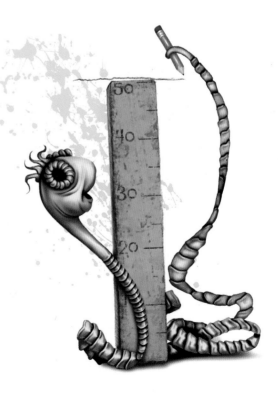

For some reason, Arthur turned kind of pale,
and the rest of the guys went quiet. I didn't mind.
I was busy eating.

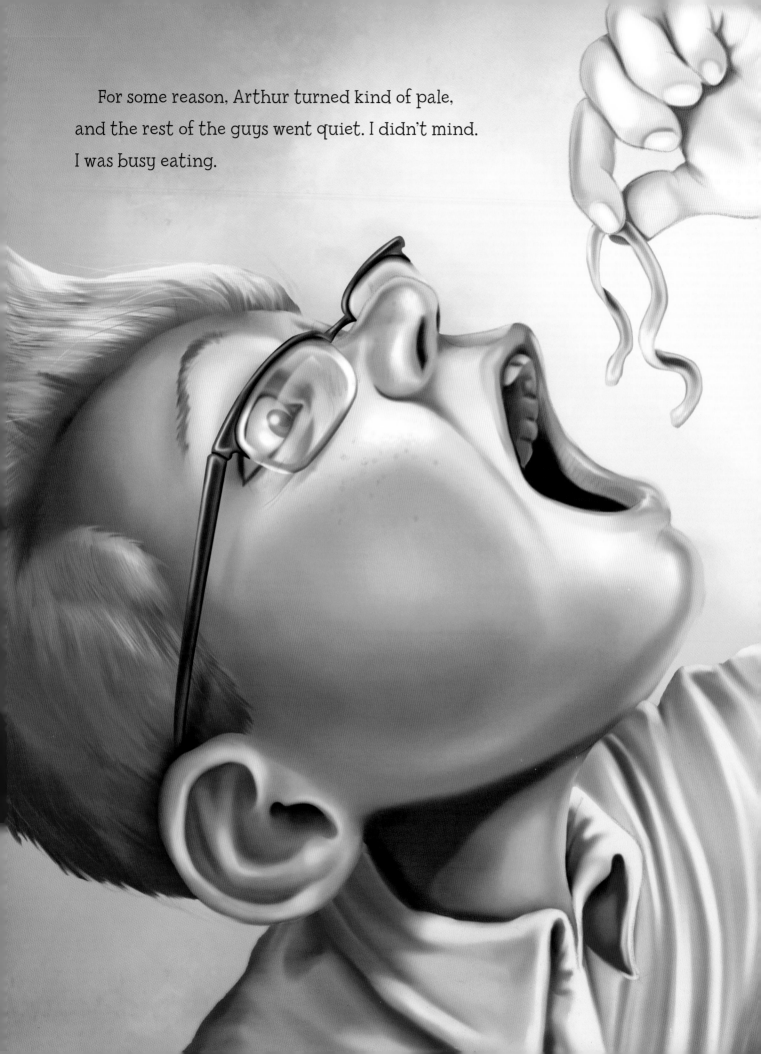

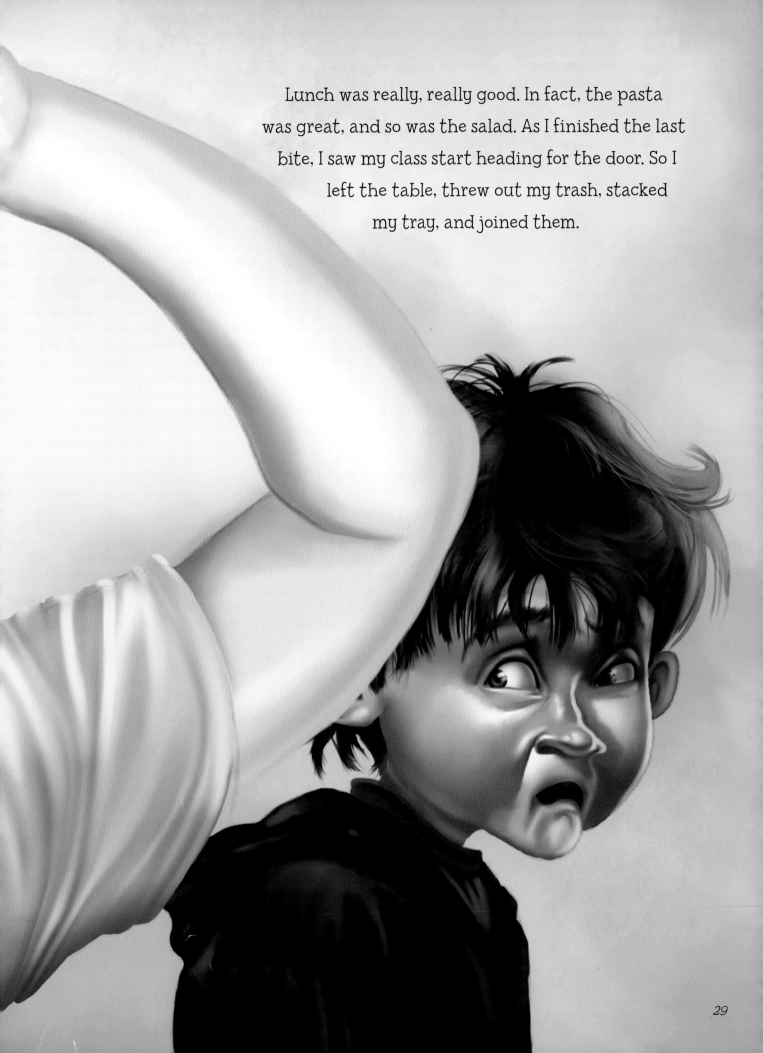

Lunch was really, really good. In fact, the pasta was great, and so was the salad. As I finished the last bite, I saw my class start heading for the door. So I left the table, threw out my trash, stacked my tray, and joined them.

29

The rest of the day was no big deal. When I got on the school bus to go home, Ginny was waiting for me. She opened her mouth to speak, but before she could say a word, I held up my hand.

"Don't even ask," I said. "I broke every single rule you gave me, but somehow I managed to survive. Plus my stomach was pretty happy. So from now on, I'm going to follow . . ."

RULE EIGHT:

Never, absolutely NEVER, pay attention to Ginny's list of SEVEN RULES YOU ABSOLUTELY MUST NOT BREAK IF YOU WANT TO SURVIVE THE CAFETERIA. Enjoy your lunch. The food is very good.

"Really?" said Ginny.

"Really," I said. "Especially the worms."